At Thompson Brook School . . .

No nut-free options. No dairy-free options. It's as if they don't want kids with allergies to eat!

These vending machines are the pits.

Well, thank *that* lady.

Hey, guys. I was wondering if we could . . . uh . . . talk.

Milmoe, we're not going to let you rub it in our faces that you won the class election.

No, it's not like that! Hector, you should've won. I'm in way over my head and I need your help!

But how could *we* even help you?

What is this?! Comic books are strictly forbidden!

And worse, you wrote this yourself?

Everyone knows creative writing doesn't fit into the educational standards stated in Code 359. The three of you will join Mr. Milmoe in the principal's office.

But what did we do?

You are disrespectful.

Well, well, well.

How very interesting to see you all in my office.

It's a shame that you're having trouble adapting to the new rules set by our wonderful new superintendent.

As you know, Dr. Van Grindheimer fired that old windbag Hernandez and appointed me as principal for a reason. Because I don't mess around.

You don't use breath mints, either.

After school . . .

Psst. Hey, kids. You want yah school back?

Huh?

Later that afternoon . . .

I don't know what Grease Burger can do to help us, but at least the Super Meals come with cool toys.

Welcome to Grease Burger, home of the Greasetacular Burger. May I suggest you mega-size your Super Meal today?

Betty! It's us—Hector, Terrence, and Dee!

Oh, hey, Breakfast Bunch. You three are a sight for sore eyes.

Betty, we need your help. Things are bad back at school.

Sorry, kids, not interested.

They're *real* bad.

Can I take your order?

WHEREABOUTS OF ESCAPED CONVICTS ARE UNKNOWN

It's them!

gulp

Wha? Where? What are you guys doing in my kitchen? Is my kitchen at school? Betty, how much time do we have until the first lunch bell rings?

Lunch Lady, the new superintendent fired us.

And Mr. Edison broke out of jail and was appointed principal of Thompson Brook.

And worst of all, Edison is trying to expel us!

And remember his evil cyborg? Well, that's our new vice principal! Our teachers have all been replaced with felons!

Peas and carrots! Well then, it's up to us to stop him! We'll need to break back into the Boiler Room and gain access to our gadgets.

But how?

With the help of an old friend . . .

It looks like somebody was trying to bust in, but they weren't successful.

Thank goulash! Quick! Before anyone sees us!

RUMBLE

Meanwhile, the Breakfast Bunch make their way to school.

Meanwhile, back in the Boiler Room . . .

Betty, get me all the intel you can on this superintendent. Why would she appoint a convict to be principal? I wanna know what makes this woman tick. Let's find out what she eats for breakfast, lunch, and dinner.

You got it, boss. . . .

Oh my. Hard-boiled egg for breakfast. Hard-boiled egg for lunch. And for dinner—a slab of steak, cooked rare.

Just as I feared, a tough cookie.

No. Doesn't look like she eats sweets. Here's her résumé. Uh-oh.

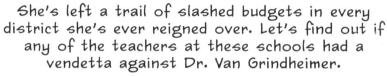

She's left a trail of slashed budgets in every district she's ever reigned over. Let's find out if any of the teachers at these schools had a vendetta against Dr. Van Grindheimer.

Hmmm. Only one problem. None of the schools listed in her résumé even exist. And her college degrees—all fabricated! The colleges she claims to have graduated from are fictitious!

Great tuna taco! She's devised a ruse to become a superintendent. But why *our* district? Pull up some surveillance footage, Betty.

In other words, it'll be Armageddon!

And that dastardly diva has been harvesting the energy from you kids. Those exercise machines in the gym are powering the whole contraption.

So that explains the weird cables attached to each treadmill.

Lunch Lady, how are we going to stop her? The school is swarming with her goons.

Betty, break out every gadget we have. Kids, rally the student body. It's time to play with our food!

We can't do this alone.

So you're with us?

At exactly 2:15, we take action!

I need to tell you something about our old lunch lady. . . .

These look like regular bananas, but they're not.

Ready, set . . .

Whisk
Whackers

It's GLORIOUS!

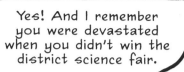
Yes! And I remember you were devastated when you didn't win the district science fair.

My project on lasers was ahead of its time!

But you didn't take home the trophy, did you?

That rat fink Hernandez did. His lunar project was as stupid as the foam moon he made. My project was science! His was just a simple craft!

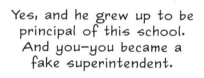
Yes, and he grew up to be principal of this school. And you—you became a fake superintendent.

wink

I told you not to come any closer!

AGHHH!

WHHSOOOM!

Spatu-copter

WHAT?!

And I remember you always loved . . .

But, Sally, don't you remember that time you forgot your lunch money?

You were crying. I didn't hesitate for a moment to give you a free lunch. Do you remember what we had that day?

BRRRII||||O|||INNG!

OK, kids, off to class with you.

Thanks for breakfast, Lunch Lady!

You've got it, kids! Work hard today. See you at lunch!

FOR MY LITTLE GIRLS, ZOE AND LUCY

The author would like to acknowledge the color work in this book by Joey Weiser and Michele Chidester.

THIS IS A BORZOI BOOK PUBLISHED BY ALFRED A. KNOPF

Visit us on the Web! randomhouse.com/kids

Educators and librarians, for a variety of teaching tools,
visit us at RHTeachersLibrarians.com

Library of Congress Cataloging-in-Publication Data
Krosoczka, Jarrett.
Lunch Lady and the schoolwide scuffle / Jarrett J. Krosoczka. — First edition.
p.   cm. — (Lunch Lady ; 10)
Summary: Lunch Lady and Betty have been fired but the Breakfast Bunch convinces them to return
and stop the school's new superintendent and her minions from carrying out an evil plan for revenge.
ISBN 978-0-385-75279-4 (trade) — ISBN 978-0-385-75280-0 (lib. bdg.) — ISBN 978-0-385-75281-7 (ebook)
1. Graphic novels. [1. Graphic novels. 2. Schools—Fiction. 3. Revenge—Fiction.
4. Mystery and detective stories.] I. Title.
PZ7.7.K76Lur 2013
741.5'31—dc23
2013004886

The text of this book is set in Hedge Backwards.

The illustrations were created using ink on paper and digital coloring.

MANUFACTURED IN MALAYSIA

January 2014

10 9 8 7 6 5 4 3

First Edition